First American Edition 2010
Kane Miller, A Division of EDC Publishing

Copyright © by Hakibbutz Hameuchad Publishing House and by Yona Tepper,
Published by arrangement with The Institute for The Translation of Hebrew Literature.

For information contact:
Kane Miller, A Division of EDC Publishing
P.O. Box 470663
Tulsa, OK 74147-0663
www.kanemiller.com
www.edcpub.com

Library of Congress Control Number: 2009932398

Manufactured by Regent Publishing Services, Hong Kong
Printed September 2010 in ShenZhen, Guangdong, China
1 2 3 4 5 6 7 8 9 10

ISBN: 978-1-935279-36-5

Written by Yona Tepper   Illustarted by Gil-Ly Alon Curiel

Translated by Dr. Deborah Guthman

Passing By

Kane Miller
A DIVISION OF EDC PUBLISHING

Yael likes to see what's going on in her street.

Who's going for a walk? Who's far away? Who's coming closer?

Here comes a little dog, wagging his tail.
He turns around, he jumps and barks, "Bow-wow."

Where's the little dog now?

Where has he gone?

He barked, "Bow-wow," and then he ran away!

Yael peeks between the railings.

Who's that in the flowers? Who's creeping so quietly?

It's a cat! She was hiding in the yard.
"Miaow, miaow." She'd like some milk.

Where's the cat now? Where has she gone?
She called, "Miaow, miaow," and then she ran away.

Yael looks down at the street below. Who's walking away?
Who's coming closer?

There's a red car driving down the street.
It stops at the light and honks its horn. What a loud noise!

Who made that noise? Who honked its horn, "Beep beep?"
It's the red car. It honked its horn and then it drove away.

Yael peeks between the railings.
Who's that whistling and ringing
a bell? Is he far away?
Is he coming closer?

It's a man, riding his bike.

He has a basket and a fishing pole, and he's wearing boots.

Where is he going? What will he do?

Where's the man?
Where has he gone?
He rang his bell, "Dring dring,"
and rode away.

Yael looks down on the street below.
Who will come by next?
A cat? A dog? Another person?

It's a little tractor with a yellow ladder.
It rumbles and rattles and drives down the street.

Where's the tractor? Where has it gone?
To pick up branches and leaves in the park?

Yael looks all around.

Who chirped? Who whistled? Who's that singing?

It's a little bird picking up seeds.

It's hopping and pecking and searching for crumbs.

Where's the little bird gone?
Where did she go?
She chirped, "Tweet tweet,"
and flew away.

Yael peeks between the railings.
She looks down onto the street.
There's no car. There's no little dog.
There's no bird. No one is coming
or going.

Wait! Who's that walking and waving?

Who is calling, "Hello! Hello!" Who looks so cheerful?

It's Daddy!

"Let's go for a walk!"